85438

D0008334

Annie Pitts, Swamp Monster

Annie Pitts, Swamp Monster

Written and illustrated by

Diane deGroat

SeaStar Books

NEW YORK

SEASTAR BOOKS
A division of NORTH-SOUTH BOOKS INC.

First published by Simon & Schuster Books for Young Readers, 1994.
Published in 2001 in the United States by SeaStar Books, a division of North-South Books Inc.,
New York. Published simultaneously in Canada, Australia, and New Zealand
by North-South Books, an imprint of Nord-Süd Verlag AG, Gossau Zürich, Switzerland.

Library of Congress Cataloging-in-Publication Data is available.

The art for this book was prepared using pencil.
The text for this book is set in 13-point Palatino.
ISBN 1-58717-044-2 (RTE)
1   3   5   7   9   RTE   10   8   6   4   2
ISBN 1-58717-045-0 (PB)
1   3   5   7   9   PB   10   8   6   4   2

Printed in the U.S.A.

For more information about our books, and the authors and artists who create them,
visit our web site: www.northsouth.com

Contents

✫　✫　✫

Annie Pitts, Swamp Monster

CHAPTER ONE

The Creature from Miss G.'s Class

Finally. After three videos and four bowls of Count Chocula cereal, my research on movie monsters was just about done. All morning I had been watching people screaming and running away from spaceships and dinosaurs and some weird thing from the Black Lagoon.

I needed to make a scary costume, so Grandma picked up some monster movies for me at the video store—old black-and-white movies from the 1950's. I couldn't believe how fake the monsters looked back then. The Creature from the Black Lagoon and the Thing from Outer Space were obviously tall men in rubber costumes. And Godzilla looked like a giant radio-controlled robot. But Grandma thought they would be good references for me.

Nowadays, movie creatures look so real, they can scare the pants off you. I'm not allowed to see the really good ones though, because I'm only nine, but I've seen the previews, and those were scary enough. I still get nervous whenever I have to go down to the basement in our building to get the laundry. There are always strange noises coming from under the stairs, and if monsters are hiding anywhere, it's usually under the basement stairs.

I know something must be there because

every load of laundry comes back with one missing sock. Mom says that the dryer eats it, but I'm not about to wait around to see a one-footed creature sneaking through our laundry basket just to prove her wrong.

So far, the only monster I've ever really seen is the one who sits next to me in class. His name is Matthew McGill, and he sure acts like he comes from another planet.

Last week he changed the words on my spelling homework when I was in the girls' room. He turned "breath," "unselfish," and "Brazil" into "dogbreath," "fishface," and "Bra." He also changed my name at the top of the paper to "Arm Pitts" but Miss Goshengepfeffer—or Miss G., as she lets us call her—knew that it was my paper anyway, and I had to write each misspelled word ten times.

My grandma said Matthew acts that way

because he likes me. I think he's just plain weird.

In fact, the only good thing about him is that he has a brother in high school who makes videos. When I heard he needed a swamp monster for one of his films, I volunteered. That's why I was doing all this research. I wanted to be the best monster I could possibly be.

Of course, I would rather have a more glamorous role for my first movie, but from what I've seen so far, the women who star in these monster movies spend most of their time screaming and fainting. Forget it. The monster is really the star, and I, Annie Pitts, am going to be the star of the movie.

And after I have a chance to show everybody what a great actress I am, then I can get other jobs too, like TV shows and commercials. I think it would be so cool to have everyone watching me as I smile into the camera and tell them to try new Golden Glo shampoo.

They'll say things like, "Didn't she play the swamp monster in that McGill movie? I didn't notice that her hair was so beautiful!"

I watched my reflection in the TV as I tossed my beautiful hair, first to the left, then to the right. And then I noticed the credits rolling by at the end of *The Creature from the Black Lagoon*.

I was sure Matthew's brother would want to use credits at the end of his movie too, so I wrote down some of the important ones. Next to "Director," I wrote "Mark McGill," because it was his movie. Next to "Assistant Director," I wrote "Annie Pitts." He'll probably need my help.

Then I wrote in large letters: "THE ROLE OF THE SWAMP MONSTER IS PLAYED BY ANNIE PITTS, FAMOUS ACTRESS." Then, next to the mummy, I wrote in very small letters: "Matthew McGill."

That was the only bad thing about this acting job. Matthew was going to be in the movie too. Mark is calling his movie *Daughter of Swamp Monster Meets Son of Mummy,* so I guess he needed Matthew to be the mummy. I hope it's a small part, though. Maybe the mummy could just scream and faint when he meets the swamp monster. Matthew should be able to handle that.

I sat up straight on the sofa and looked at my reflection again. I didn't really think the swamp monster was going to have to do a lot of smiling, but I needed to practice for those other jobs I would get after Mark's movie.

My mother came into the living room just as I was doing one of my most difficult smiles—smile #3—the one where just the top teeth show, and the corners of my mouth turn up a little.

Mom was not impressed. "You're still in front of that TV?" she asked. "What about your homework? Don't you have a biography due Monday?"

"I'm doing research," I answered.

She picked up one of the videotapes. "And whose biography are you doing? Godzilla's?"

"The tapes are part of my research for Mark's movie," I explained. "I need ideas for my costume before we start shooting this afternoon."

Mom handed me my backpack and said, "I think you have time to squeeze in some homework before you go."

I, in turn, gave her smile #12, the one that says, "I'm-going-to-start-it-right-this-minute-and-thank-you-for-reminding-me."

I rummaged through my pack, still smiling that same smile. That seemed to satisfy my mother, and she went back into the kitchen to do whatever she was doing before she interrupted my research.

Except for a candy wrapper and a Burger Barn key chain, the only thing in my bag was a book I had taken out of the school library yesterday. It wasn't a biography. It was a book called *Myths, Monsters, and Mysteries.*

I opened to the chapter on swamp monsters and saw a drawing of a creature described by a Mrs. Luella Blinsinger of Palm Beach, Florida. She swore on a stack of Bibles that she saw this monster near Lake Okeechobee around Easter of 1974. Apparently, it was never seen again. Not even by Luella. . . .

The drawing in my book showed a tall hairy creature covered with scales. That's exactly what I wanted for my swamp monster costume.

Tall might be a problem for me, though. After all, I was only in fourth grade. But I could be scaly, and I could be hairy.

I brought the book into my room and closed the door. I put on my artichoke costume my grandmother had made for the school play last month. The green leaves sort of looked like scales.

Hairy was no problem either. My curly red hair stuck out all over the place, just like my mother's and my grandmother's. The three of us live together, and sometimes people say we look alike.

Of course, we don't look exactly alike. My mother's red hair is mostly gray, and my grandmother's red hair is neon orange because she dyes it.

Well, this swamp monster was going to be as hairy as I could make her. I bent over so my hair hung down toward the floor. Then I sprayed it with a whole can of hair spray and waited for it to dry.

As I was waiting, the blood was rushing

to my head. When my lips felt like they weighed about ten pounds each, I stood up. In the mirror, I could see that my face was as red as my hair, and my hair was as big as a house.

Unfortunately, I didn't look like a swamp monster.

I looked like a troll.

Obviously, I needed to work more on my costume.

CHAPTER TWO

Mean and Green

I didn't want to look like a troll. I wanted to look like a scary monster.

Then I remembered that the Creature from the Black Lagoon had webbed hands and feet. I dug through the closet until I found my old swim flippers that I used in the town pool last year. The problem was that I had put on the artichoke costume before putting on the flippers, and believe me, it's not easy trying to bend over and put flippers on when you're a big puffy vegetable. I was barely able to get the toes of my sneakers in just far enough.

Unfortunately, the flippers were bright pink. Pink was my favorite color last year. My clothes were pink. My room was pink. Even my toilet paper had to be pink. So, of course, my flippers were pink too. I really didn't think a swamp monster would have bright-pink feet, though. Maybe a troll would. But not a swamp monster.

I took out the can of hair coloring left over from Halloween and sprayed my flippers a lovely shade of neon green.

I also sprayed the tops of my sneakers and the floor all around my feet. When I stepped away, there were two flipper prints inside a circle of green. It looked kind of cool, but I didn't think my mother would think so. I pulled the rug over it.

Just in time, too, because I heard my

mother's footsteps coming down the hall. When she got to my door, she said, "Annie, I made you a sandwich. Can I come in?"

My mother was trained not to come into my room whenever there was a DO NOT DISTURB sign on the knob. I left it there all the time.

"Don't come in," I said. "I want to surprise you."

"Okay," she said. "I'll leave it out here."

Lunch would have to wait until I finished my costume. I shook the can again and sprayed my hair. I could still see some red, but the tips were nice and green.

My face was pasty white, now that the blood had drained out, so I sprayed some green color onto my hands and rubbed it all over my face.

There was still something missing, though. I wished I had another pair of flippers for my hands. But maybe I had something even better.

Grandma once bought me a package of fake fingernails at a garage sale. Mom wouldn't let me wear them to school because she thought I might accidentally poke someone's eye out. They were perfect for my costume, though, because they looked like claws.

I peeled off the back of each nail and stuck it onto my own. You were supposed to trim them down, but I left them nice and long. And Ruby Red. After all, I was a female monster.

The nails were kind of dressy, so I thought I might as well go all the way and add some earrings. I had humongous gold clip-on earrings that Grandma gave me to play dress-up when I was little. They were just what I needed to give the swamp monster that extra elegant touch. Now all I needed was some slime.

I peeked out of my bedroom door. My mother was back in the kitchen, and Grandma was out. I flip-flopped out into the hall, stepping right onto the tuna salad sandwich my mother had left outside my door. Part of it stuck to the bottom of my right flipper. It was slimy, all right, but it wasn't what I had in mind.

I peeled the squished tuna sandwich off my foot, flip-flopped across the hall to the bathroom, and flushed it down the toilet. Then I searched for some real slime.

I knew that my grandmother had a bottle of super-smelly shampoo called "Mountain Moss" in the medicine cabinet. She called it "earthy-smelling," but I thought it smelled more like rotten garbage—a perfect smell for a swamp monster.

I poured some of the Mountain Moss onto the tips of my scales. It oozed and dripped down, making dark smelly splotches all over

the green felt. Now I was ready. I was mean and I was green. And I was slimy and smelly too.

The doorbell rang, and then I heard Mrs. McGill and my mother talking in the living room. They were planning to go shopping after dropping us off at Tibbetts Brook Park. Because we don't have any swamps in our neighborhood, Mark decided to shoot the movie in the woods there.

I opened the bathroom door just as Mom was coming down the hallway to get me. We stood face-to-face. She was looking at a swamp monster, and I was looking at a woman with a very weird expression on her face.

"Annie!" she finally said. "You look . . . awful!"

"Thank you," I answered. "I'm supposed to. I'm a swamp monster."

"Well, you certainly smell like one," she said.

I gave her smile #7—the one that says, "Aren't-you-proud-to-have-such-a-talented-daughter?"

I flip-flopped past my mother, down the hall, to the living room. Mrs. McGill was standing by the front window. When she saw me, she didn't even act surprised like my mother did.

Instead she said, "You look great, Annie. Mark's going to love the costume. The boys are waiting in the car, so you go ahead. Your mom and I will be down in a minute."

Gee. I was hoping for more of a reaction. I guess when you have a kid like Matthew, you're used to seeing gross stuff all the time. I thanked her anyway and headed out the door.

My whole life was about to change. After this movie, I would no longer be Annie Pitts, plain kid.

I would be Annie Pitts, FAMOUS ACTRESS!

CHAPTER THREE

The Road to Fame

We live on the second floor of a two-family house, so I had to flip-flop my way down to the front door. All the way down I wondered if anyone, besides my mother, would ever believe that inside this artichoke costume was the Ever-Dreadful Swamp Monster.

Certainly not Matthew. As soon as he caught sight of me, he shouted from the car window, "What're you supposed to be— moldy broccoli?" I ignored him. Nine-year-old boys can be so immature.

Mark was much more grown-up. "Looks great," he said.

"But she's wearing earrings!" Matthew said. "Swamp monsters don't wear earrings!"

But Mark didn't seem to mind. He leaned over Matthew and opened the car door for me. I was lucky to have such a mature high school person like Mark for my first movie director. When I go on talk shows, I'll mention how he helped me get started in show business.

I climbed over the mummy and sat in the middle seat. "Hey, Slimeball," Matthew said, "don't sit next to me. You stink!"

"I'm supposed to stink," I said. "I live in a swamp."

I was about to say that Matthew stank too, but then I realized that he actually smelled good. He smelled like the Burger Barn, my favorite place for hamburgers. Then I saw the ketchup that Matthew had poured all over his mummy costume to look like blood.

Mark got up and said, "I'll take the middle seat. Annie, you can sit by the other window. I don't want my costars fighting. Not yet, anyway. Save that for the movie."

Mark was so nice. I'm sure he wished he were my brother instead of Matthew's.

We switched seats, which wasn't easy because one of my flippers got caught on the camera case. The other came off somewhere between Matthew's elbow and Mark's right knee.

"Watch it!"

"Sorry."

"Ouch!"

"Sorry."

When I was finally seated, I said to Mark, "You will be pleased to know that I've practically memorized every scene from *The Creature from the Black Lagoon.* Only I've decided that in our movie, the swamp monster shouldn't die at the end because we may want to do a sequel—I know *I* will—also, I made a list of credits. Here. What do you think?"

I flashed the list in front of Mark's face. Mark just stared blankly at the paper while Matthew groaned and banged his head against the window.

"Never mind," I said. "Can I have my script now? I'd like to go over my lines."

"Script?" Mark said.

"*Script,*" I repeated. "*Script.* What am I supposed to say? What am I supposed to do? And how exactly do I kill the mummy?"

Matthew yelled, "Forget it, Slimeface! The swamp monster gets it in the end." He made a karate chop across Mark—"Hee-yah!"—just missing my knee.

"Nobody dies," Mark said calmly. "And nobody gets a script. I'll tell you what to do

and when to do it. I have it all worked out. Up here." He pointed to his head. I could see the director was going to need my help after all.

Our mothers finally joined us and we drove off. The ride was pretty quiet, which was good because I needed to psyche myself up for my role as the swamp monster. I really wanted to do a good job.

I looked at my reflection in the window and experimented with all kinds of scary monster faces. I stuck out my teeth and squished my eyes shut. I tried to pretend I was no longer Annie Pitts. Instead, I was DAUGHTER OF SWAMP MONSTER!

When I opened my eyes, I discovered I was making scary monster faces at a passenger in the car next to us. An old man was staring back at me.

I hope I didn't scare him too much. I didn't

want him to have a heart attack and go to the hospital and tell everybody that a green scaly monster was threatening the city of Yonkers.

But the man suddenly did something I didn't expect. He laughed. He laughed hard. All the way to the next light.

What was wrong with my costume? At this point I wished I was the mummy instead of the swamp monster. You couldn't mistake a mummy for a vegetable or anything else. Even the worst mummy costume would look like a mummy. A couple of rolls of bandages and some ketchup. Bingo. You're a mummy.

Well, I worked very hard trying to look like a scary monster. I was green and I was slimy. And I smelled really bad. What more did they want?

I was about to find out.

CHAPTER FOUR

Let's Give Her a Hand!

As soon as we got out of the car, Mark headed straight for the woods, with Matthew right behind him. I tried to follow too, but with the flippers on, I could barely keep up. Not to mention that my hair kept getting caught in the branches along the muddy path.

"Did anyone bring a mirror?" I asked. "Or a brush?"

"Oh, brother," Matthew said. I guess that meant no.

"Didn't you guys bring anything?" I asked. "What about a tape player? Don't we need scary music playing in the background?"

Mark started walking faster and said over his shoulder, "Stop worrying. I have everything we need."

"Well, I know something about movies," I said, "and I know you need stuff like music and lights and directors' chairs . . ." I stopped to catch my breath. I guess Mark was so far ahead, he couldn't hear me. He stopped only when he got to the top of the hill.

When I caught up with him, I could see that he and Matthew were looking down into a dark, muddy ditch. "What's that?" I asked.

"The swamp," Mark announced.

Matthew started down the hill with his backpack bouncing over his shoulder, while I stood next to Mark, ready to help.

"I'm going to take a shot of that ditch for the first scene," he explained. "That'll give the movie just the right feeling—dark and mysterious." He set up the tripod.

"Ah, dark and mysterious," I repeated. I looked over his shoulder as he looked through the camera. He sounded really professional. Maybe he would know some famous directors or producers that I could interview for my biography project. Then after I interviewed them, I could audition for any parts they might have for a talented person such as myself.

I was about to ask him, when he shouted, "Matthew, get out of there! There's no mummy in this scene!"

Matthew climbed back up the hill and Mark turned the camera on and filmed the swamp monster's "home."

"Maybe you should get a close-up of that log down there," I suggested.

Mark stopped filming and turned to me, saying, "Annie, this video camera has sound. Do you know what that means?"

"Of course I know what that means. I'm an actress. I know all about cameras."

Matthew started laughing so hard, he almost fell back down the hill.

Mark didn't think anything was so funny. He said, "If you know anything about video, Annie, then you should know that it picks up every word you say when you're standing near it. I would like the opening shot of the swamp to be silent. I don't want to hear talking in the background."

"*Sorrr-rrry,*" I said.

"*Sorrr-rrry,*" Matthew said, imitating me.

Mark filmed the swamp again. The very quiet, silent swamp. Then he said, "Okay, Annie, this is going to be your first scene. We'll start out with the swamp monster rising up out of the ditch."

I had a better idea. "What if the camera first zoomed in on my hand, like in *The Creature from the Black Lagoon*? I think that would be a good beginning to the movie," I told him. I held up my Ruby Red claws and turned my wrist gracefully so Mark could get a good view.

But Mark just said in a low, steady voice, "I know what I want. And I want the swamp monster rising up out of the ditch. We're meeting the swamp monster for the first time, and I think it would be more exciting if we shot the whole monster at once."

I certainly wanted my first scene to be exciting, so I said, "Okay. If that's the way you want it. What would you like me to do?"

Mark said, "Get behind that log down there, and then slowly stand up. And make a scream of some kind."

"Why should I scream?" I asked. "Just because I'm a girl monster doesn't mean I have to go around screaming. Let the mummy do the screaming."

"Okay, Okay." Mark sighed. "You don't

scream. You . . . yell. Yes, you yell and howl like a monster who's really mean and scary. How does that sound?"

"Better," I said. "But exactly what kind of yell should I make?" I asked, trying to sound professional.

"You can yell any way you want to," Mark answered, still looking through the camera.

"But you're the director. Should I yell like I'm angry, or just sort of crazy-like?" I wanted to get it just right.

Mark stuck his face into mine. "Just yell!" he yelled. "Now get going. We don't have all day! It's going to start raining any minute!"

"All right," I said. "I'm going."

I wiggled my way down the hill as carefully as I could, holding on to rocks and roots to avoid slipping in the mud. I finally reached the log, but it was half buried in the gushy, gooey mud. My flippers made a slurpy noise as I stepped around it. Yuck. I didn't think acting was going to be this gross.

"Get lower so I can't see you," Mark shouted.

I squatted daintily.

"I can still see you," he said, looking through the camera. "Get all the way down!"

"It's too muddy," I answered back.

"Of course it's muddy. It's a swamp!" Mark shouted.

I guess I had no choice. I lay down on my stomach. My face was almost in the mud. I was trying not to think about how gross it was.

I tried to think about how I would rise up from the swamp. What emotion should I have? Should I really yell, or should I just have a mean look and sort of growl a little?

What I did do was gasp, because suddenly I spotted something weird right next to me. It was a hand. A bloody hand sticking up out of the mud.

"*AAAAAAAAAAAARGK!*" I screamed. I jumped up, tossing mud in all directions.

"*AAAAAAAARGK!*" I screamed again, tripping my way up the hill.

"*AAAAAAAARGK!*" I screamed at Matthew and Mark. I couldn't get any words out, so I pointed to the swamp. Then I pointed to my hand.

But Mark was still pointing the camera at me the whole time. "Perfect!" he said. "And cut!"

"But there's a dead body down there!" I finally managed to say.

"You mean a hand," Matthew said, leaning against a tree, smiling.

"You saw it?" I shouted. "I can't believe we're making a movie in a swamp with a dead person in it!"

"Calm down," said Matthew, laughing. "It's not real. I put it there. It's only plastic."

"Plastic!" I screamed. "*Plastic?*" I lunged at him.

"Hold it! Hold it!" Mark came between us and said, "It was my idea. I wanted to make sure the monster was scary-looking when it came up out of the swamp. And believe me— you were!"

"Well, you could've asked me to *act* scary," I said. "That's why I'm here. I'm an actress! I'm supposed to *act*."

Mark shrugged his shoulders and said, "I wasn't sure you could do it."

"You should've given me the chance," I said, still angry.

"Don't worry. You'll get one," he said. "We're going to do the scene now where the swamp monster and the mummy meet."

Matthew took his karate pose and hopped toward me, chopping the air. "I'm ready," he said. "Hee-yah!"

CHAPTER FIVE

Getting the Willies

Matthew chopped the air a few more times with his bandaged mummy hands, but Mark pulled him back and said, "Stop fooling around, Matt. I want to get this done right." Then he explained what we were going to do next.

"We'll shoot the next scene at the playground. Annie, you'll creep up on some unsuspecting kids, and pretend to grab one or two of them. Then the mummy comes along and tries to take them away from you. This will be the first time the mummy and the swamp monster meet."

"I'm supposed to grab kids?" I asked, surprised. "Won't they be scared?"

"That's the idea," Mark said, packing up the camera. "I want them to look really frightened, just like you were when you saw that fake hand. Remember—it's only pretend."

I wasn't sure I liked Mark's way of scaring people. But I had to admit, it worked on me.

I followed the boys along a path that led to the playground. Unfortunately, it was such a nasty day that the playground was empty, except for a little boy playing in the sand. His mother was reading on a bench under a nearby tree.

We watched them from the bushes. "There's nobody there except that little kid,"

I said. "He's practically a baby. I can't go scaring a baby."

But Mark said, "It's for the movie. Remember, you're an actress."

I still wasn't crazy about the idea, but I went along. I guess an actress has to do what she has to do for her career.

We hid behind a tree while Mark said, "Remember what I told you, Annie. I want you to sneak up behind the kid, scream real loud, and pretend to grab him. Then the mummy sneaks up from the other side and does the same thing. Both of you hold on to him while I shoot from back here."

"Hey, wait a minute," I said. "What about his mother? She's sitting right there."

"I'll explain everything to her afterward," Mark said.

Mark seemed to have everything under control, so I prepared myself for my big scene. I was finally going to do some real acting!

When Mark gave me the okay sign, I crept as quietly as I could toward the boy. I had to lift my flippers up real high with each step so they wouldn't make any noise. I raised my arms over my head too, because I figured that's how a monster would walk.

Along the way, I turned my head to make sure the camera was on me. And when I was sure that it was, I gave it my best smile— smile #1. This was the smile that was going to get me into toothpaste and lipstick commercials, and any other commercials that needed a professional smiler such as myself.

I was so busy looking at the camera that I wasn't watching where I was going. I walked right into the wall of the sandbox. My flipper got caught under it and I lost my balance. But just before falling face-first into the sand, I, Annie Pitts, remembered to say my line:

"*AAAAAAARGK!*"

Of course, the little boy jumped sky-high

and screamed. When Matthew suddenly leaped out of nowhere and yelled *"GRRRRRK!"* the boy jumped sky-high and screamed again.

Then everything happened at once.

The boy's mother came running toward us, shouting, "What do you kids think you're doing? Get away from here! I'm going to call the police!" She picked up the screaming toddler and tried to comfort him, but he was a goner. I wished that Mark would hurry up and get here to straighten things out.

Meanwhile, Matthew tried to calm the boy down by taking off some of the mummy bandages that were wrapped around his head. "Hey, look," he said with a goofy smile. "I'm not really a mummy. I'm just a kid. See?"

Since I thought Matthew was still gross-looking, with or without bandages, I was surprised when the boy actually stopped crying. I wanted to help too, so I said, "And I'm not really a swamp monster either. I'm really an artichoke!" I danced around with a stupid smile on my face. One that I would never, ever, use in front of a camera. The kid burst out crying again. I wished that Mark would hurry up and get here to straighten things out.

This wasn't fun anymore. I didn't like the idea of being this kid's worst nightmare. He'll probably grow up being afraid of artichokes for the rest of his life.

He could be in a restaurant someday, and a waiter will pass by with a plate of artichokes, and the kid will start screaming bloody murder. Everyone will think that he found a cockroach in the food, and they'll all get up and leave and put the restaurant out of business.

And it will all be my fault.

Finally, Mark came out of the woods carrying the video camera. "I'm sorry your little boy got scared," he said in a sweet voice that I had never heard him use before. It must be the one he uses with grown-ups.

"Willomina's a girl," the woman said sharply.

Mark didn't miss a beat. "And she's a real sweetheart too," he said.

He smiled at the woman and continued, "I'm making a movie for my film class at school. These are my actors, Matthew and Annie. And this little bo—girl must be a professional model. She's a real cutie." To me, she looked more like a cootie.

"Oh, no," the woman said. "She's never modeled. But everyone says Willy is so cute, she should be in the movies."

Mark asked if he could film the cootie,

I mean cutie, some more, and Willy's mother was delighted. He filmed the kid jumping off the bench. Ten times. Then he took some shots of her throwing sand all over Matthew and me. Mostly me.

I went along with it just so Willomina's mother wouldn't call the police. I was glad it worked, because if we got arrested, I'd have to go to jail in this monster costume and have my mug shots taken—front and side view—with mud and green stuff all over my face.

I'd also have to invent a new smile for the mug shot.

One that says, "It's-not-my-fault-they-made-me-do-it."

CHAPTER SIX

Slimebreath Meets Fungusface

After Willomina and her mother left the playground, Matthew climbed to the top of the monkey bars. He pounded on his chest and yelled, "Hey, Mark, take my picture up here!"

But Mark said, "Get down from there. We're going over to the baseball field. We need more room to shoot the fight scene."

"Awwww-right!" said Matthew. He came chopping toward me, but Mark stopped him.

"Cut it out, Matt!" he said.

"Yeah, watch it," I added. "You might get hurt."

Matthew put up his karate hands again and said, "If anyone's going to get hurt, it's going to be the moldy broccoli!"

"No way," I said. "Swamp monsters are stronger than mummies."

"Says who?"

"Says me."

"Oh, yeah?"

"Yeah!"

That was the way our conversation went all the way to the baseball field, where we continued to "Oh, yeah" each other until our noses were about two inches apart. We would have been closer, except my puffy costume was in the way.

Being this close to Matthew gave me a whole new view of him. For instance, I never noticed the row of little brown hairs sticking out between his eyebrows. Or the gaps in his mouth where his baby teeth had fallen out. Or the veins in his neck that stuck out when he got really mad. Or . . .

Ooof!

Matthew karate-chopped my stomach. It didn't hurt, because I was so well-padded, but he did manage to knock me off my feet. Right into the mud puddle at first base.

"Ha!" he boasted. "The swamp monster is history!"

That's what he thought. I grabbed his leg and pulled him into the mud with me.

And so the fight scene began. Sort of. I rolled on top of Matthew and tried to pin him down, but I was so round, I rolled right off again.

"*Wait!*" Mark yelled from across the field. "*I haven't set up the camera yet!*"

We didn't wait. Matthew and I were mud wrestling. I mean, we wrestled more with the mud than with each other. Every time we tried to get up, we slipped back into the mud. Matthew finally managed to stand, but I was stuck facedown in the mud.

"Ha!" Matthew sneered. "The swamp monster eats dirt!"

"I'm almost ready!" Mark shouted. *"Hold on!"*

I didn't hold on. I stuck out my flipper and tripped Matthew, sending him once again into the puddle.

Matthew was getting mad. He shoved me with his feet and rolled me over. Now I was stuck on my back with my flippers waving all over the place.

Matthew grabbed my foot, and the flipper came off in his hands. "I win, Slimebreath!" he shouted.

"One more second!" Mark yelled.

"Hey! Gimme back my fin, Fungusface!" I yelled. I reached out and grabbed a handful of bandage from Matthew's leg. I tugged hard and the mummy fell forward——arms, legs, and flipper flying in all different directions.

His head landed right next to mine. Suddenly something inside me made me do something I never expected to do.

I bit his ear.

"Owww!" Matthew yelled. "No fair biting!" He rubbed his ear and tried to get up. But it wasn't easy. Like me, he had become part of the mud puddle.

"Okay! I'm ready!" Mark shouted. "Action!"

Matthew waved to his brother and said, "Wait! Did you see that? She bit me! She touched me with her tongue! That's disgusting!"

This, of course, was coming from a kid who is famous for licking worms if someone dares him to.

"Don't worry about it, Matt. Let's start that scene all over again. It was great, but I wasn't ready."

"No way. I'm done," Matthew said. And then he shouted to the world, "Annie Pitts is disgusting!"

I sat up. "What's disgusting is this mud," I said. "What are we going to do now? Our costumes are ruined!"

Mark looked at his watch and said, "I don't think we have time to do any more shooting anyway."

"But what about the movie?" I asked. "How does it end? It has to have an ending." I managed to stand up and make my way onto the grass.

Mark put the camera into the case and said, "It doesn't have to have an ending, Annie. It's just an assignment for my film class. It's really not that important."

"It is to me!" I said.

"Who cares?" Matthew whined. "I'm cold, and I'm hungry, and I want to go home so I don't have to look at your ugly face anymore."

"We can't go anywhere," I said. "Look at us!"

Matthew and I were completely covered with mud. Maybe Matthew didn't care, but I couldn't go home looking like this.

"Go see if the bathrooms are open," Mark said. "Maybe you can get cleaned up in there."

The town pool was back near the playground. It was closed for the winter, but the bathrooms and showers were still open. I headed for the ladies' locker room.

All Matthew had to do to get clean was to take off his bandages. I, on the other hand, couldn't take my costume off. I was wearing only a turtleneck shirt and a thin pair of tights underneath. And my Minnie Mouse underpants showed right through the tights. I decided I would just have to clean up the artichoke costume as best I could so I could wear it home.

I stepped under the shower and tried to turn the handle, but it wouldn't budge. I forced it as hard as I could, and suddenly a blast of cold water hit me. By the time I could turn it off, I was soaked from head to toe.

But in the mirror I saw that I was actually clean. Wet, but clean. The mud was gone. But something strange was happening.

The Mountain Moss shampoo had suddenly started to bubble.

CHAPTER SEVEN

Home Again, Home Again

"**G**ross!"

That's what Matthew said when he saw me. I was a walking ball of suds. And if I smelled bad before, that was nothing compared to the aroma now oozing from my costume.

Mark backed away, saying, "Get rid of that thing! It's disgusting—even for a swamp monster!"

"I can't take it off," I said. "I don't have

anything else to wear. Can you lend me your jacket?"

"No way! You'll mess it up," he said.

"Then I'll just have to go home like this," I said. "But if I mess up your mother's car, it's all your fault."

"All right, all right," he said. He lifted his windbreaker over his head and handed it to me. "But try not to smell it up too much," he added.

"I'll try," I mumbled, and I went inside to change. It wasn't easy getting out of the costume. Two of my fake fingernails were loose and popped off while I was struggling with a knot.

I left the two nails and the bubbling costume in the trash can of the ladies' room at Tibbetts Brook Park. I put on Mark's jacket, and was glad that it covered most of me up.

And so we walked out to the bus stop to

wait for our ride: Mark in his T-shirt, Matthew in a Spiderman pajama top, and me in a size large windbreaker that came down to my knees.

We must have looked pretty weird waiting at the bus shelter. Matthew sat on one side of me, and two teenaged girls sat on the other. Mark stood out by the curb with his back to us. I guess he didn't want the girls to know he was with a couple of fourth-graders.

It started to rain harder, but Mark stayed right where he was, getting soaked. No one on the bench talked. It was sort of like being in an elevator. For some reason, people don't talk to each other at bus stops or in elevators.

It reminded me of the time I burped in the elevator on the way to the dentist's office, and it echoed really loudly. My mother was embarrassed, but I wasn't. I thought it was funny. But I was little then. If I had to burp in

an elevator now, I would probably try to hold it in.

The teenaged girls didn't talk and they didn't burp. But they were noisy anyway, because they snapped their chewing gum. I don't know how they make that loud cracking noise without blowing bubbles. I think you learn it in junior high.

I couldn't help but notice that the girls were wearing fake fingernails also. One had Ruby Red, just like mine. The other had a peachy color.

I sat with my hands folded gracefully over my knee. I tucked in the fingers with the missing nails and sat up tall. Maybe they would think I was in high school too. After all, I was wearing a high school jacket. And humongous gold earrings.

I tried to think of a way to start a conversation. Maybe I should tell them I was an actress and I had just completed my first movie. That would impress them.

A car suddenly pulled up in front of the bus shelter. It wasn't Mrs. McGill's car, but Mark got in anyway.

"Hey!" Matthew yelled after him. "Where're you going?"

Mark shouted back through the rain, "Tell Mom I went to the Burger Barn with Mike and James. I'll get a ride home later."

Matthew ran out to the car. "Can I come too?" he yelled through the half-opened window.

"No! You guys keep an eye on the equipment and wait for Mom. She should be here any minute. And anyway, you're wearing your pajamas!"

Matthew came back under the shelter and slumped down onto the bench, pretending he didn't know me. Fine. I didn't want the girls to think I hung out with fourth-graders either.

I was about to mention how immature that boy on the other end of the bench was, but they had already started talking to each other. In between gum snaps, I realized, they were talking about Mark.

"So, what'd ya think?" *snap* "Cute?"

snap "Nah, too skinny."

"Nice hair, though." *snap*

"Couldn't tell." *snap* "It was wet."

"Maybe it's"—*snap*—"mousse."

snap "No way." *snap, crack, crack*

I was so fascinated by all that snapping and cracking that I didn't notice at first when the girl next to me offered a piece of gum.

"Wanna piece?" *snap*

"Sure!" I said. I couldn't believe a real high-school person offered me gum! I unwrapped it and popped it into my mouth. The girl reached over and offered Matthew a piece too, but he was busy wiggling his tooth and ignored her.

Then the girls started talking about Mark again.

"I think he's in my"—*crack, crack*—"math class."

"Ooooooooh"—*snap*—"lucky you."

My gum was just about soft enough and I tried to make it snap—*sst.* All I could make was a slurp sound. I tried again—*chk.* This was harder than I thought.

I was about to ask them to teach me how to snap gum, when the bus came and they jumped in. Suddenly, Matthew and I were left alone on the bench.

He was busy wiggling one of his loose teeth, and I was busy trying to snap my gum. It was clear that we weren't ever talking to each other again.

The cracking and the wiggling continued until I noticed a strange figure coming toward us. Through the rain, I could just make out someone carrying a large beach umbrella. There were cows printed all over it. The figure also carried some shopping bags, a skateboard, and a tangled bunch of rope.

There was something very familiar about this person. In fact, there was only one person I knew who would carry an umbrella like that.

"Grandma!"

CHAPTER EIGHT

Very Interesting People (VIPs)

Grandma scooted under the shelter, closed her cow umbrella, and said, "Annie! Matthew! What are you two doing all alone out here?"

"We're waiting for Mom and Mrs. McGill to pick us up," I said. "Mark already left." Before I could ask her what she was doing at the bus stop, she squished herself and all her belongings onto the bench between Matthew and me.

"Oh, good," she said. "I can hitch a ride

back with you kids instead of taking the bus. Whew! Nasty day, isn't it? Lucky for me, I picked up this umbrella at a garage sale down the street. Do you have any more gum, Annie? I'm starving."

"You can have mine," I said. "It doesn't work."

"What's it supposed to do?"

"I'm trying to make it crack," I told her. "But I can't figure out how to do it."

Grandma said, "I don't think I can help you there. Did you ask Matthew if he knows?"

"We're not talking to each other," I explained as I poked through the shopping bags. Grandma often came home with interesting things from garage sales. "What's in here?" I asked.

"Oh, someone was selling a bunch of nice kids' books. I'm going to give them to the school library."

She rummaged through the bags, pulled out a paperback, and said, "Here's one you might like, Matthew: *Under the Mummy's Spell.*"

Matthew started looking through the book, while Grandma checked out the rest of her "treasures." She held up the skateboard. "You know, I've always wanted to try this. Maybe you kids can teach me. And here's a perfectly good fishnet. I was thinking of making a spider costume for Halloween. This could be the web. The seniors at the center where I volunteer will love it."

Grandma finally settled back and said, "So, where are your costumes? I didn't get a chance to see you all dressed up before I left."

"It's a long story," I groaned. "I'll tell you later."

"But how did the shooting go?" she asked.

"Okay," I said.

"Just 'okay'?" she asked. "You mean I don't have a wonderful new monster film to look forward to?"

Matthew was surprised and asked, "You like monster movies?"

"I like the old ones." Grandma laughed. "Last night we rented *The Creature from the Black Lagoon, Godzilla,* and *The Thing from Outer Space*—just so Annie could get some ideas for your brother's movie. Now those are real classics!"

"Wow!" said Matthew. "My grandmother only lets me watch Disney movies."

"We still have the tapes," Grandma said. "You can come over and watch them if you want to. Ask your mother."

"He can't come over," I said quickly. "We have too much homework."

Matthew said, "What homework?"

I stuck my gum under the seat and said, "I'm not talking to you, remember?"

Matthew turned to Grandma and said, "Would you please ask Annie what homework we have to do? I was at the orthodontist yesterday afternoon and didn't get the assignment."

Grandma looked interested. "You're getting braces, Matthew?"

"When all my baby teeth are out. See?" He pulled back his lips to show my grandmother all the baby teeth he still had left.

"I see," she said. Then she turned to me and said, "Matthew would like to know what homework you have. He was absent yesterday."

"I know," I answered. "I had a very pleasant afternoon. Tell him we have to do a biography project for Monday."

"Annie says you have a biography project due on Monday."

"Ask her what we're supposed to do."

"Matthew wants to know more about the project."

"I don't remember. Something about choosing someone we know and making a presentation about them in front of the whole class. Tell him that Miss G. kept saying she wanted it to be interesting. That's all I remember."

Grandma turned to Matthew. "Did you get that?"

"Sort of. Ask her if it's an oral or a written report."

"Oral or written?"

"Let me think . . ." I said. I tried to remember what Miss G. had told us. I should've paid more attention. "I think we can do it any way we want to," I said. "As long as it's some kind of presentation. She said we can work with partners too. That much I remember."

"Isn't that lovely, Matthew? You can work with a partner."

"Tell her I don't want to be her partner."

"Tell him I didn't ask him."

"Well," Grandma said. "Now that that's all settled, suppose you tell me whose biography you're doing, Annie."

"That's the problem," I said. "I can't think of anybody. Do you know any interesting people, Grandma?"

"Well, let's see," she said. "There are some fascinating people at the senior center. Like Gus Wicki. I think he's interesting. He used to be the voice of Pepi Le Cat."

"Who's Pepi Le Cat?" I asked.

"Pepi is an old cartoon character from many years ago," she said. "Gus also sang the song in the Sudso commercial. You know, the one that went, *'A little Sudso makes a lot of suds. Use it safely on your delicate duds.'*"

"Wow!" Matthew said. "You know someone famous!"

Grandma laughed. "I might know some other interesting people too."

And so Grandma gave us a whole list of interesting people she knew, beginning with all the kids she tutored at the Y, and ending with an eighteen-year-old pilot named Dennis.

"How do you know a pilot?" I asked.

"He's my flying instructor."

"Your flying instructor!" I yelled. "Grandma, you're taking flying lessons?!"

"Yes, but don't tell your mother. She's such a worrywart. In another three months I can get my pilot's license. Then I'll take you for a ride. You too, Matthew."

"Thanks!" he said. "I bet you're the only grandmother in the country who flies a plane!"

Grandma laughed. "I'm not so sure about that," she said. "But I do know that I'm the only grandmother in the painting class at the college downtown."

I suddenly realized there was a lot I didn't know about my grandmother, and what she did when I was in school. "I didn't know you took painting lessons," I said.

"I don't," she answered. "I'm the model. Some of the students are quite good, you know."

That sounded interesting. Maybe I could do it myself someday, if I'm not too busy making movies. "Do you get to wear fancy costumes and stuff?" I asked.

"No," she said matter-of-factly. "I don't wear anything at all."

Matthew's jaw dropped and I coughed suddenly and almost choked, but Grandma just kept on talking about her modeling job.

"And you know what's interesting?" she said. "The instructor says she prefers older models because they have more character."

I quickly changed the subject by saying, "Speaking of character, we still have to choose one for our biography. Ask Matthew who he's doing."

Grandma turned to Matthew. "Annie wants to know whose biography you're doing."

Matthew thought for a minute, then said, "I don't know anyone as interesting as you, but I have an idea. I'm thinking of doing a biography on monsters."

I didn't like the way that sounded. "What are you talking about? I mean—ask Matthew what he's talking about."

Grandma turned to Matthew and said, "Matthew?"

Matthew answered, "The mummy and the swamp monster are interesting characters. Tell her I'm going to bring in Mark's video-tape that we made today. That way I don't have to do anything for homework."

"But I'm on that tape!" I shouted. "Tell him I want to use it for my project too!"

"Well, well," Grandma said. "Looks like you're partners after all!"

CHAPTER NINE

Presenting . . .

When I got to the classroom on Monday morning, Matthew handed me a large yellow envelope with a note scribbled on the outside. It said, "Send to Producer."

"What's this?" I whispered to Matthew.

"I swiped this from Mark's room after he left this morning. It must be the edited tape."

"But look," I said, pointing to the note. "Is Mark really going to send it to a movie producer?"

"I guess so," Matthew said.

"Is that what he said?"

"I didn't ask him."

"How could you not ask him?" I said a little too loudly.

Miss G. raised her hand to get our attention. "Boys and girls," she said, "we have a lot to cover today. We want to give everyone a chance to present their biographies. I know you've worked very hard on this project, so I expect some wonderful *blah blah blah . . .*"

While Miss G. talked, I was thinking about movie producers watching our tape. It must have turned out really good if Mark was sending it. This was definitely the beginning of my acting career! I jumped up with excitement. "Yes!" I shouted.

Miss G. called on me. "Annie, would you like to go first?"

I suddenly realized I was standing. "Uh, no,

not yet," I said and sat down. Matthew and I had agreed we wanted to do our presentation last because we knew it would be the best one.

Miss G. called on Susan, and Susan walked to the front of the room with poster board under her arm. When she placed it on the blackboard tray, I could see that there were photographs of firefighters glued all over it. I noticed that one of them was a lady.

Susan cleared her throat and began. "My biography is about Linda Brown, a firefighter with the Yonkers Fire Department, Engine Forty-seven. She's also my mother."

Her report was very interesting. She told us about the dangerous things that firefighters have to do, and how she worries about her mother sometimes when she's at work.

Miss G. thanked Susan for her great presentation and called on Thomas to go next. Thomas had bragged on Friday that he was going to interview the president of a toy company.

He said his father plays golf with him.

Thomas didn't have any pictures. He just read from his paper:

"Mr. Ralph Butts is the president of the Fun Time Toy Company.

"His office has a gray rug and pictures of boats on the walls. He talks a lot on the phone and drinks a lot of coffee.

"I asked him if he got any action figures for free, and if he had any extras, because I really liked them. He said he didn't.

"I asked him what new toys were coming out. He said he didn't know. Somebody else did that.

"I asked him what he did. He said that he watched the money.

"I asked him if I could help him watch the money. He said no.

"I asked him if he liked kids, and he said not really.

"The end."

I heard a few giggles from the back of the room.

Miss G. hushed them and said, "Thomas, that was . . . interesting. But could you tell us a little more about Mr. Butts' life? Did you learn how he got started in the business?"

Thomas looked at his paper to see if there was anything there that he had missed. There wasn't. "He wasn't nice at all," he finally said, almost in tears. "I thought a toy company would have nice people in it!"

"Well, thank you for the report, Thomas," Miss G. said. She sent him gently back to his seat. "Now who would like to go next?" No one raised his hand, so Miss G. volunteered some kids.

We heard about a piano teacher, a truck driver, and an uncle who was an orthodontist. Ayuko told us about her older sister, who only ate white food—like potatoes, spaghetti, and vanilla ice cream.

Right before lunch, Miss G. called on Marsha. "Oh, please let me go last," Marsha-the-Wonderful said sweetly, "because mine's the best one." She folded her hands neatly on her desk as she spoke.

"Well, Marsha," Miss G. said, "if we have to have one more biography before lunch, then it should be the best one. Who are you reporting on?"

Marsha walked to the front of the room and said, "Myself!"

No kidding. Marsha did her own biography. She talked about how she had won a beauty contest when she was three years old, even though most of us have already heard that story.

She talked about her horseback riding lessons and how she's going to get a riding outfit for her birthday. She also talked about the skirt she was wearing that she had bought yesterday just for this presentation.

She didn't even read from a paper. I guess she knew everything about herself by heart. And now we did too.

Miss G. said she wasn't sure if Marsha followed the directions or not, because she couldn't remember saying that we couldn't write our own biographies. That would make it an autobiography. Miss G. is very strict about following directions. She thanked her for her very thorough report, and sent us all to lunch.

In the afternoon, we listened to a few more presentations, and then Miss G. called on Matthew and me to make the last one. Finally, everyone was going to see my first movie—including me!

Matthew jumped up and popped the tape

into the VCR. I thought we needed some kind of introduction so I stood up and said, "Matthew and I did something very interesting. We took two of the most interesting characters we could think of, and we made an interesting presentation about them. I hope you like it. It's very . . . interesting." Then I sat down.

Miss G. smiled at us, and I could see she was happy that we had made a video. She had borrowed the VCR from the library, hoping that someone would need it.

Everyone watched the screen. Suddenly a redheaded swamp monster came screaming toward the camera.

"What's that supposed to be?" Thomas shouted. "A troll?"

"No! It's a swamp monster," I said. "It doesn't look anything like a troll!"

But just then the swamp monster tripped,

and everyone laughed. I remembered when that happened. It was right after I saw the fake hand, and I was trying to climb back up the hill. Mark was supposed to cut that part out of the tape.

Then the swamp monster tripped again.

And again—this time in slow motion. Why would Mark edit the tape this way?

The next scene was a super close-up of the swamp monster's mouth saying, "Try Golden Glo shampoo. Try *Golden* Glo shampoo. Try Golden *Glo* shampoo."

It was me, practicing my smile, while Mark and Matthew went off to move some branches that were in the way of the camera. I was just standing around, so I tried out all my different smiles right into the lens. Smiles #1 through #12. But I didn't know the camera was running at the time! "What's going on?" I asked Matthew.

"I don't know," he said. He picked up the envelope and a letter fell out. As he read it, Matthew had a strange look on his face. "Uh-oh," he said. I grabbed the letter and read:

Dear Sir:

Enclosed is some material that I think would be perfect for your show, America's Funniest Halloween Bloopers. *If you choose to show it, please send payment to the above address.*

Thank you.
Sincerely,
Mark McGill

CHAPTER TEN

Smile! You're on Candid Camera!

I couldn't believe that Mark put this stupid tape together! Things I had done when I thought no one was looking were now being shown to the entire class—and soon to all of America, if Mark had his way.

The camera even caught me trying to do the moonwalk with my flippers on. The way they were laughing, you'd think the class had never seen a swamp monster do the moonwalk before.

I was really mad now. "Where's the rest

of the tape?" I shouted to Matthew over the noise.

"I don't know," he said. "Mark probably took it to school with him." Then he laughed and added, "But this is pretty funny!"

He stopped laughing suddenly when the mummy appeared on the screen, picking his nose. Believe me, it wasn't easy for a mummy to pick his nose when it was covered with bandages, but Matthew managed to find a way.

Then we saw him wiggling his butt. I guess that was Matthew's imitation of me trying to climb down the hill. We saw the butt wiggle two more times in fast motion. Everyone thought that was hysterical. Even Miss G. was laughing.

Matthew buried his face in his hands, but I sat and watched the whole thing, unable to take my eyes off the screen. I was finally in a movie, and it had to be the most humiliating experience of my life.

And finally, when I was sure there couldn't possibly be any more embarrassing moments, the camera zoomed in for a lovely view of Annie Pitts lifting up her costume to pull up her tights. Now everyone in Miss G.'s class knows that I wear Minnie Mouse underpants. This was the worst thing that had ever happened to me. The second worst thing happened next.

Miss G. wiped her eyes with a tissue and said, "I must say that in all my years of teaching, I've never seen a biography done so . . . so . . . creatively! But I'm afraid you two didn't follow directions. The assignment was to present information about a real person. You've chosen to present some fictional characters. I'm sorry, but I'll have to give you each a zero."

Matthew jumped up and cried out, "Well, I didn't know it had to be a real person! Annie didn't tell me that! She said we could do it on

anybody as long as it was interesting! It's all her fault."

Miss G. was not giving in. "If you were absent, Matthew, you should have gotten the assignment from someone else. Someone reliable."

Then Miss G. looked at me and said, "We went over this material quite thoroughly, Annie. You were probably daydreaming again."

Miss G. waited for me to say something, but I didn't know what I was supposed to say. After all, she was right. I chewed on my fingernail and stared at the wall, the flag, the doorway. And that's when I spotted Grandma, walking down the hall with two large shopping bags full of books.

"Miss G.!" I said quickly. "I'm sorry you didn't like our video, but that wasn't our official biography. Matthew and I will present the *real* one right now."

Matthew looked at me. "We will?"

"Of course. Just like we planned. First the monster tape. Just for fun. Then the real one."

"The real one?" Matthew said.

"Yes," I said. "But first I have to get our visual aid."

"Our visual aid?" I wished Matthew would stop repeating everything I said and go along with me.

"I'll be right back," I said and sped out the door. Matthew and the rest of the class were surprised when I returned with Grandma, shopping bags and all.

"This is our visual aid, Miss G.," I said. I stopped to catch my breath, hoping that Matthew-the-Stupid would catch on. I finally saw something in his brain click.

"Oh, yes, our visual aid," he said loudly. He came up to the front of the room and stood next to Grandma and me. Then he whispered, "What exactly are we doing?"

Grandma answered for me. "I think we're doing my biography," she whispered.

I spoke out of the corner of my mouth as I smiled out at the class. "Just go along with me, you two, and everything will be cool."

I started my speech. "Our biography is about my grandmother, Isabel Quinn. She's a real live Very Interesting Person."

"Very interesting," Matthew repeated.

"Yes, very interesting," Grandma said also.

"She takes care of me when my mother works, but when I'm in school, she does some amazing things. Like . . ." I paused, waiting for Matthew to continue.

"Oh," he said. "Like she takes flying lessons. She's going to get her license." Finally, Matthew was getting it.

I continued, "And she does a lot of volunteer work at the senior center where she knows a lot of interesting people like . . ."

"Like Gus Wicki," Matthew said. "He's famous, because he used to sing the Sudso commercial. He did a cartoon voice-over too. Mrs. Quinn is going to get his autograph for me."

This is going great, I thought. I went on, "And she helps out a bunch of art students by . . ."

"By taking all her clothes off," Matthew said.

He was supposed to talk about Grandma tutoring at the Y. Not about the painting class. I didn't think the whole class needed to hear about my grandmother being naked.

"She's a model," I explained. And then I quickly added some other things, like her garage sale adventures—how she finds really neat stuff like skateboards and Ruby Red fake fingernails, and books for the library, and I stopped only when I couldn't remember anything else.

When we were finished, there was still some time left over for questions. The kids were especially interested in the flying lessons. "But nobody tell my mother," I said. "She doesn't know."

They asked if Grandma could get Gus Wicki's autograph for them too. Grandma said that she would see what she could do, and then the bell rang, and suddenly it was time to go.

Miss G. thanked Grandma for being our visual aid, and she thanked us for giving a proper report. Matthew and I smiled at each other with a look that said, "Whew-that-was-close."

Then we remembered that we weren't ever going to talk to each other again, unless we really had to—like in class—and he walked one way and I walked the other.

But before I left the classroom, I tossed the tape into the trash can. I wanted to be in a movie, but not as a tripping, moonwalking, no-pants swamp monster!

As we walked home, Grandma said, "I'm sorry the film didn't work out the way you had planned. But you and Matthew handled it pretty well."

I scuffed my sneaker across the sidewalk and said, "Yeah, but I'm still never talking to him again."

Grandma hugged my shoulder and said, "You know, you'd have a nice friend there if you gave him half a chance."

I made a face and said, "Actually, I think he likes you better than he likes me."

"Does that bother you?" Grandma asked.

"I'm not sure," I said, because I really wasn't.

"Well, I'm sure about one thing," Grandma said. "You could use some cheering up, Annie. How would you like to go to the Burger Barn for a shake and some fries?"

We never went to the Burger Barn except

on Wednesday nights when my mother worked late, so this came as quite a surprise. "I think a large order of fries would make me feel a whole lot better," I said. "And maybe a hamburger too."

"Sounds good to me," Grandma said, smiling.

So my show-business career was kind of off to a slow start. But I once heard about an actress being "discovered" by a movie producer while she was hanging out in an ice-cream place. Who knows? Maybe someone could get discovered at the Burger Barn. Sometimes they take pictures of people for their posters.

Maybe I should work on a new smile just in case. . . .

Read all of the books about
Annie Pitts!

Annie Pitts, Artichoke

An *American Bookseller* "Pick of the Lists"

"Annie manages to create havoc with surprising results. . . . A fun book for middle readers."
—*American Bookseller*

"Amusing and highly palatable reading fare, with sprightly, realistically drawn illustrations that enhance the book's energy and fun."
—*Booklist*

Annie Pitts, Swamp Monster

"This entertaining sequel to *Annie Pitts, Artichoke* is sure to earn new fans for author-illustrator deGroat. The plot is wonderfully silly but believable, the dialogue is snappy and truly childlike, the black-and-white illustrations are delightful, and the short chapters will appeal to young readers." —*Booklist*

"The slapstick humor will have young readers giggling. . . . this sequel to *Annie Pitts, Artichoke* is breezy and lighthearted."—*School Library Journal*

Annie Pitts, Burger Kid

"Clever, humorous plot details . . . meld into a delightful, laugh-out-loud example of how the dramatic and highly imaginative Annie embellishes everyday life. . . . Fans of *Annie Pitts, Artichoke* and Annie's other adventures won't be disappointed." —*Booklist*

Diane deGroat,

illustrator of nearly one hundred books for children, is the author of two more riotous books about Annie—*Annie Pitts, Burger Kid* and *Annie Pitts, Artichoke*, which *Booklist* proclaimed "amusing and highly palatable . . . sprightly . . . fun." She is also the author of the popular stories about Gilbert the opossum, including *Happy Birthday to You, You Belong in a Zoo*, and *Roses Are Pink, Your Feet Really Stink*, both IRA–CBC Children's Choices.